The No-Nothings and their Baby

Anne Mazer & Ross Collins

Arthur A. Levine Books An Imprint of Scholastic Press

LIBRARY OF CONGRESS CATALOGING-IN-PUBLICATION DATA

Mazer, Anne.
The No-Nothings and their baby / by Anne Mazer;
with pictures by Ross Collins.   p.   cm.
Summary: The very dumb parents take the advice they received about their new
baby very literally.

ISBN 0-590-68049-8

[1. Babies—Fiction. 2. Parent and child—Fiction. 3. Humorous stories.]
I. Collins, Ross ill. II. Title. PZ7.M47396No   2000 [E]—dc21 99-19571

Text set in Kosmik-Bold Three. Display type handlettered by Ross Collins.
Book Design by Marijka Kostiw

10 9 8 7 6 5 4 3 2 1   0/0 01 02 03
Printed in Singapore   46
First Edition, September 2000

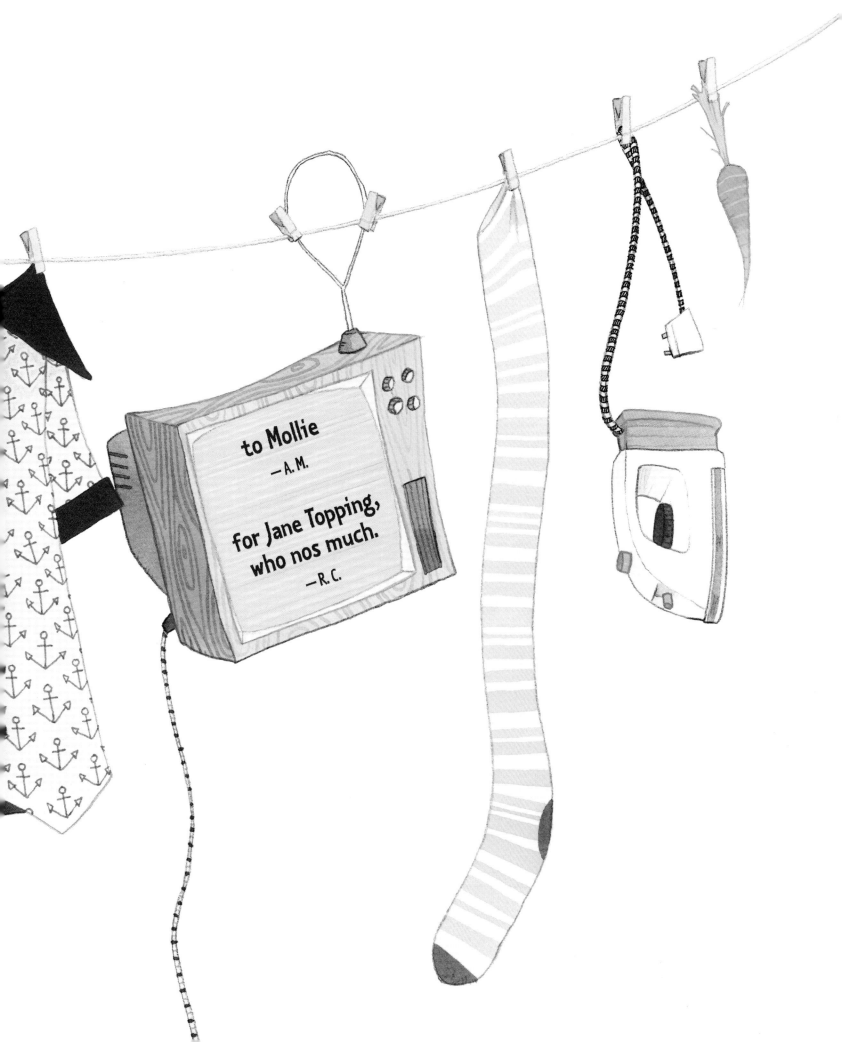

to Mollie
—A. M.

for Jane Topping,
who nos much.
—R. C.

Once upon a time,
there lived two very dumb people.
Their names were

Bertram Reliable Butternut
No-Nothing

and

Doriana Hiccup Whatsername
No-Nothing.

They were **very, very** dumb.

But they did one clever thing in their lives.

They had a daughter named Betty.

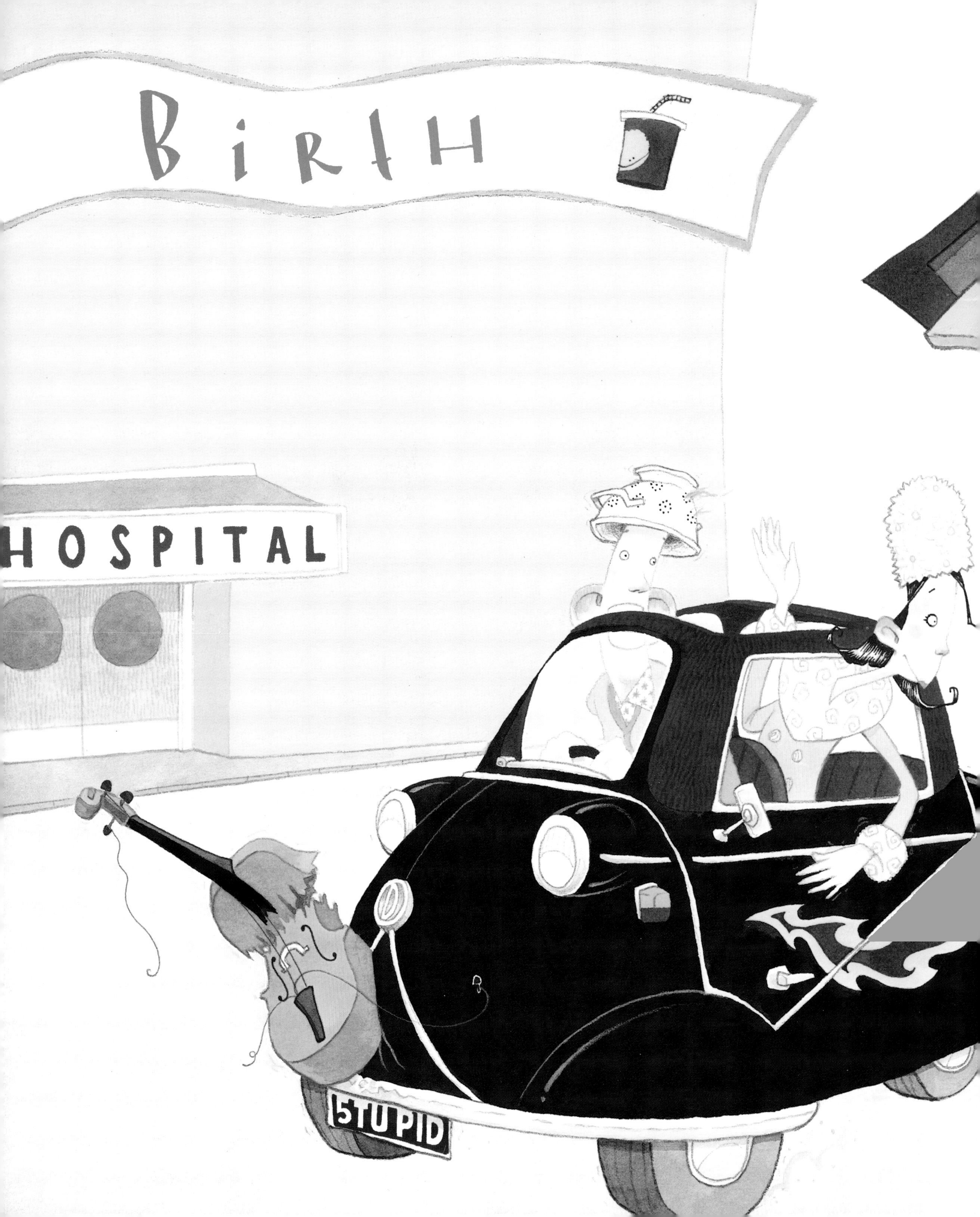

Birth
HOSPITAL
ISTUPID

"Your order, please?"

"We're here for the baby," Mrs. No-Nothing said.

"Baby??"

"Your ad said, **'speedy delivery.'"**

"Try over there," said the clerk.

"I got extra-large fries, some onion rings,
and three milkshakes, with extra ketchup
on the side," Mr. No-Nothing said.

"How smart you are, Bertram Reliable,"
said Mrs. No-Nothing. "Now we'll have food for the baby."

In the Hospital

"Do you know how to diaper her?"
the nurse asked.

"**Oh, yes!**" Mrs. No-Nothing said.

"No one can diaper like Doriana Hiccup,"
said Mr. No-Nothing.

"You're right about that!" said the nurse.

Betty started to **cry.**

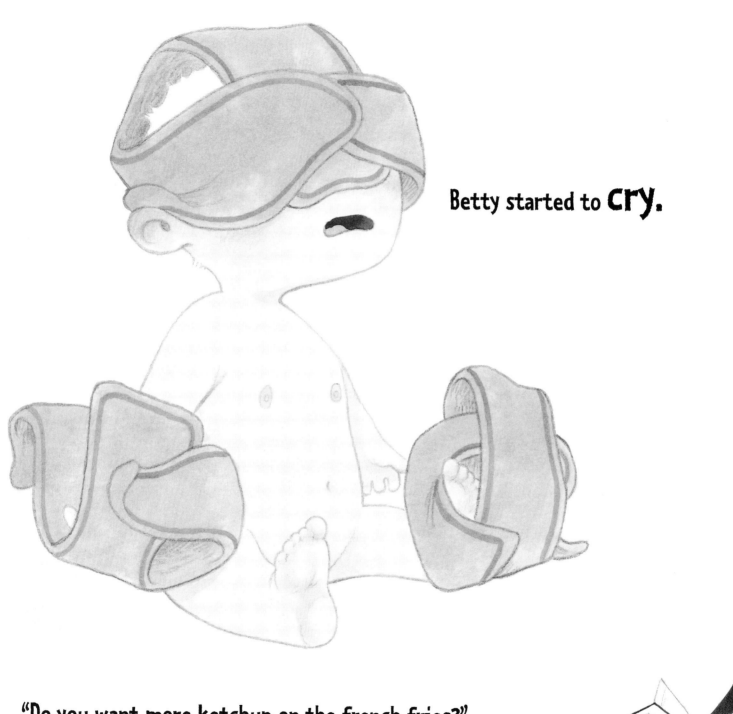

"Do you want more ketchup on the french fries?"
Mrs. No-Nothing asked.
"Or maybe you like onion rings better."

"Give her a bottle," the nurse said.

"That's what babies like."

"That looks good," Mr. No-Nothing said.

"I'll have one."

"Me too," said his wife.

The No-Nothings smiled at each other.
"Isn't this fun?"

They loved their daughter very much.

the SHoWeR

A few days after Mrs. No-Nothing and
the baby came home from the hospital,

Mr. No-Nothing announced, **"Guess what!**
I'm throwing a surprise party for you
and the baby!"

"I love surprises," Mrs. No-Nothing said.

Mrs. No-Nothing **dressed**
Betty for the baby shower.
The doorbell **rang.**

Surprise!

the neighbors yelled.

"Have some spaghetti muffins," Mr. No-Nothing offered. "I made them myself."

"Isn't it time for the shower?" the neighbors said.

Mrs. No-Nothing led the guests into the bathroom.
She turned on the water in the shower stall.

"No, no, no, no, no," the neighbors said.
"The baby doesn't go in the shower."
"She doesn't?" asked Doriana.
"No," the neighbors said. "Never."

"I know what to do,"
said Bertram Reliable.

"I'll take the shower for her!"

"**Let's open the presents,**" the neighbors said.

Just then, the doorbell rang.

"Ice-cream cake for the shower,"

the delivery man said.

"A gift from Cousin Wendy Toenail

Sassafras No-Nothing."

said the neighbors.

"Look, Bertram Reliable!"
cried Doriana Hiccup.
She brought the cake right into the shower.
Betty licked some
frosting off the
head of her
rubber duck.

"We'll always treasure this gift," said Mr. No-Nothing.
"This is the best surprise shower ever,"
his wife agreed.

Awwww!

said the neighbors.

The Walk

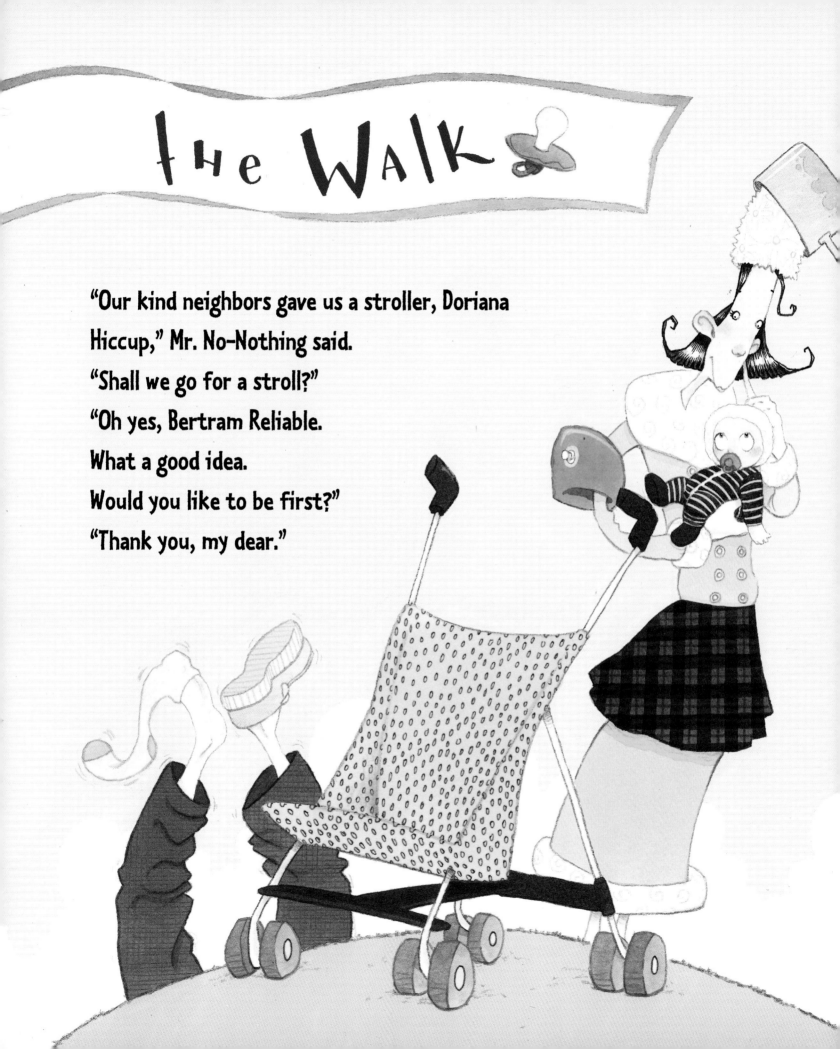

"Our kind neighbors gave us a stroller, Doriana
Hiccup," Mr. No-Nothing said.
"Shall we go for a stroll?"
"Oh yes, Bertram Reliable.
What a good idea.
Would you like to be first?"
"Thank you, my dear."

Mr. No-Nothing got into the stroller.
Then his wife climbed in and
put the baby on her lap.
**The three No-Nothings
sat in the stroller
together.**

"Isn't this fun?"
said Bertram.

"We're one
happy family,"
said Doriana.

"Why do you think
we're **not** moving?"
Mr. No-Nothing
asked.

Betty waved her little fist.

"Oh, look! The starter key!"
cried Mrs. No-Nothing.

"I'll start it!"

"Oh no, allow me, dear!"

"Gmmmfrrfff."

Betty reached for the key.

"Blllaaaach."

"Doriana Hiccup, my dear, **what a ride.**"
"Betty did it all by herself," Mrs. No-Nothing said proudly.
"Our little daughter is already smarter than us."

"Maybe she's a genius."

"It's your side of the family that's so smart, Bertram Reliable. Didn't your great-aunt count to ten?"

"Tchh, tcch, Doriana Hiccup, you were the one who graduated from kindergarten."

"That was nothing," Mrs. No-Nothing said.

"Just dumb luck. But then again,

we're a very lucky family, aren't we?"

ROUTE 0.3

to Spatulaville

S
W—e
N

Big Hill

Slightly Smaller Hill

SCALE
0   ½   1mile

ROUTE 842000

to Nostriltown

No-Nothing House

DRIVE

SUNNY

M   A

POO ST.

PLATYPUS

CRESCENT

ST.